Head, Shoulders, Knees, and Toes

Illustrated by Jeannie Winston

ALADDIN PAPERBACKS
New York London Toronto Sydney Singapore

First Aladdin Paperbacks edition July 2003
Illustrations copyright © 2003 by Jeannie Winston

ALADDIN PAPERBACKS
An imprint of Simon & Schuster Children's Publishing Division
1230 Avenue of the Americas
New York, NY 10020

READY-TO-READ is a registered trademark of Simon & Schuster.

Book design by Debra Sfetsios
The text of this book was set in Century Oldstyle.

Printed in the United States of America
2 4 6 8 10 9 7 5 3 1

Library of Congress Cataloging-in-Publication Data

Winston, Jeannie.
Head, shoulders, knees, and toes / illustrated by Jeannie Winston.—
1st Aladdin Paperbacks ed.
p. cm. — (Ready-to-read)
Summary: Children and animals act out the words to a familiar song that
teaches about body parts.
ISBN 0-689-85813-2 (pbk.) — ISBN 0-689-85814-0 (hc : library edition)

1. Body, Human—Juvenile literature. [1. Body, Human.] I. Title. II.
Series.

QM27 .W555 2003
611—dc21
2002014946

Head,

3

shoulders,

knees,

and toes,

knees

and toes.

Head,

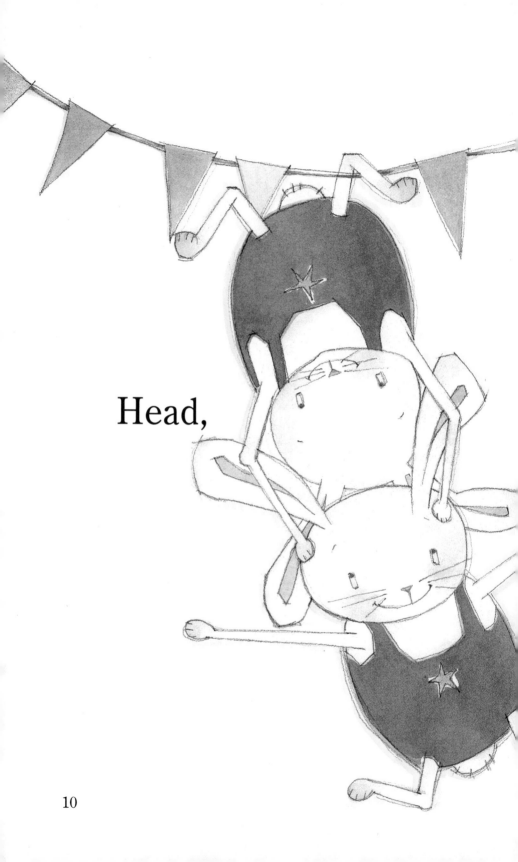

shoulders,

knees,

and toes,

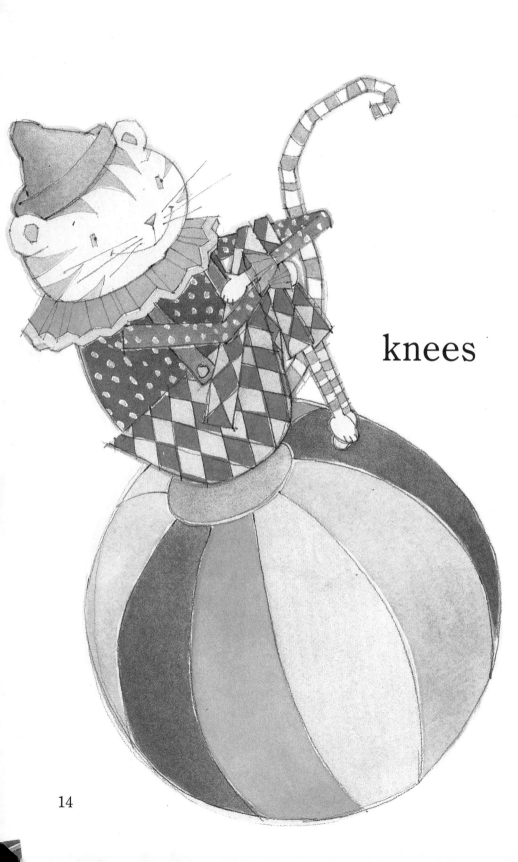

knees

and toes.

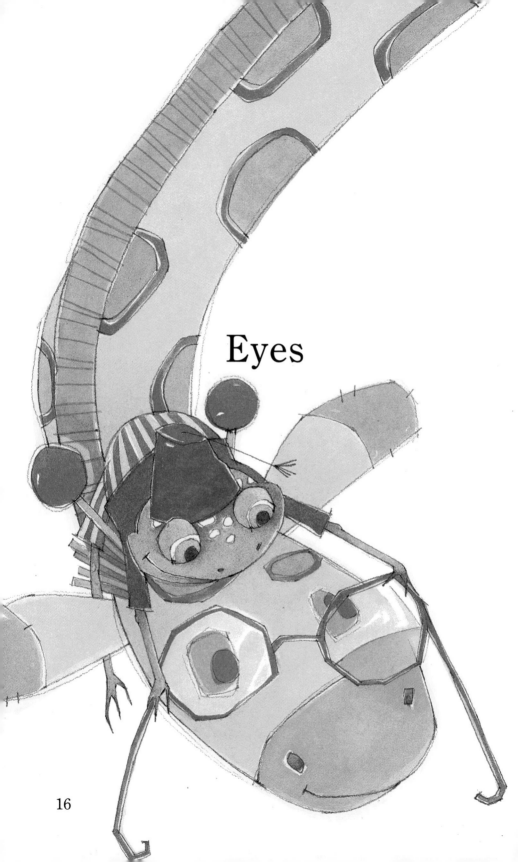

Eyes

and ears

and mouth

and nose.

Head,

shoulders,

knees,

and toes,

23

knees
and toes!